William has the brown hair and Jules the gold

THE DULCIMER BOY

TOR SEIDLER

ILLUSTRATIONS BY

BRIAN SELZNICK

LAURA GERINGER BOOKS

An Imprint of HarperCollins*Publishers*

But without another word the stranger took himself off

CHAPTER ONE

THERE WAS A STRANGER at the front door with a wicker chest under his arm.

"Tradespeople use the back," said the massive, bald-headed gentleman who answered.

Instead of turning away, the stranger handed him a card.

"This be you?" he asked.

The bald gentleman took the card. It read:

EUSTACE CARBUNCLE, ESQ.

THE CARBUNCLE ESTATE

THE HILL ABOVE RIGGLEMORE

NEW ENGLAND

Mr. Carbuncle nodded curtly but did not ask the stranger in. The stranger's curly brown hair was full of dust, and his navy-blue clothes were scruffy. He also stammered in an undignified manner: the words jerked out of his mouth as if they would have preferred staying inside him.

"This here's . . . for you then. Used to belong to your wife's sister, but your wife's sister . . . she died. A weakly creature she was, and she's . . . gone away."

"Ah," Mr. Carbuncle said, removing his hands from the pockets of his smoking jacket to accept the wicker chest. "And she remembered us in her will? Something of value, perhaps?"

But without another word the stranger took himself off, hurrying through the gate in the picket fence and down the hill.

In Mr. Carbuncle's mouth was a thick black cigar, which rescued his large pink face from suggesting a certain harmlessness. The cigar twitched at the fellow's behavior. But in a moment he turned and took the wicker chest into the house.

"Amelia, my dear," he called out. "Something from your sister."

Mrs. Carbuncle entered the hall with a weary sigh and a faint odor of disinfectant. She was a narrow, black-stockinged woman with her hair caught up in a black scarf; her narrowness and hardness of feature were in strong contrast to her husband. She leaned her broom against the banister and came over to the hall table, where he had deposited the chest.

"My sister?" she said. "But I haven't seen her these years. Why would she send us something now, out of the clear blue sky?"

"She died," Mr. Carbuncle replied. "You never know—it might be something of value."

"Oh, well then," said Mrs. Carbuncle.

They opened the lid to the wicker chest.

Inside were a tiny boy with golden curls, an equally tiny boy with hair all different shades of brown like a bowl of nuts, and a strange musical instrument. The boys were both sound asleep, and a note was wound in the instrument's silver strings. It said:

William has the brown hair and Jules the gold.
They are ten months old.
This dulcimer is all their father has to give them.

Mrs. Carbuncle crossly tore the note into little pieces. She was careful, however, to stuff the pieces into her apron pocket, letting none of them drop on the floor, for she had already done the hall that morning.

"Who even knew Molly was married?" she cried. "A wonderful wedding announcement!"

She then went to the hall closet and began to pull on a pair of galoshes. When Mr. Carbuncle asked her why, she explained, "You know how it is down there around the orphanage—all that river muck."

Mr. Carbuncle looked from his wife to the strange merchandise in the wicker chest. Beside the chest stood a pewter bowl full of unpaid bills.

"Let's not be rash, Amelia, my dear," he said, puffing thoughtfully on his cigar.

"Mr. Carbuncle?"

"It occurs to me that we've been handed a golden opportunity."

"Golden opportunity?"

"Mmm."

Mrs. Carbuncle stared aghast at the gentleman of leisure she had married.

"But, Mr. Carbuncle! You can't be thinking of taking them in! Think of the expense, sir! Think of the wear and tear on your furniture, your rugs. And we can't even afford to reshingle the roof!"

"Exactly," said Mr. Carbuncle, lifting his eyes in that direction. "Don't think the neighbors haven't noticed."

He could not see through to the roof that was in disrepair, but he could see the ceiling moldings, around which his cigar smoke was curling. They were very grand, but they were dingy in spite of all his wife's efforts. "Besides," he added, "these two won't eat much."

Mrs. Carbuncle's face grew very pinched, but she did not drop her tone of servility.

"I don't understand, Mr. Carbuncle," she said.

"Two objects of charity, Amelia. Don't you see? Two objects of charity under our roof. That's better than painting *and* shingling!"

All Mrs. Carbuncle could do was sigh.

"Oh, well then," she said.

CHAPTER TWO

THE TWO LITTLE BOYS were installed in the bedroom next to that of the Carbuncles' son, Morris. On Sunday the family went for a stroll down into Rigglemore, pushing the two boys ahead of them in a pram. It quickly became known that they had taken two objects of charity under their roof.

That evening, as every evening, Morris excused himself from dinner the instant he had finished his second dessert and took himself off to bed. He believed he grew faster lying down, fooling the pull of gravity. Although he was not yet as tall or as meaty as his father, it was his great ambition to outstrip him.

Mrs. Carbuncle served her husband his usual coffee and brandy and struck the match for his after-dinner cigar. But he neither sipped nor puffed with his usual relish.

"People seemed impressed, didn't you think?" she said, puzzled.

Mr. Carbuncle frowned, turning to William and Jules, who were squeezed into a high chair on his left.

"How old was Morris when he started to talk?" he asked.

"Why, he said 'potato' at fourteen months," she replied.

"But they're only ten months. And that one already babbles like a brook."

He pointed his cigar at William, the one with the nut-brown hair, who in fact had looked from side to side throughout the afternoon stroll, saying, "Dog." "Yellow." "Old man."

"Well," said Mrs. Carbuncle, "some children are slower than others. It doesn't mean—"

"For Heaven's sake! Morris isn't 'some child.' He's a Carbuncle!"

Turning his great, dinner-flushed face on Jules, the one with golden hair, who was nearer him in the high chair, Mr. Carbuncle said, "You don't talk yet, do you?"

Jules, who had not spoken that day, opened his mouth, closed it, then opened it again. A small, rather unintelligible sound came out. Mr. Carbuncle, having just taken a puff on his cigar, exhaled. As the thick smoke enveloped Jules's little face, his mouth closed, his blue eyes blinked in surprise.

"Black," William commented, pointing to the cloud of smoke.

The ceremony of asking Jules if he could talk and then blowing cigar smoke in his face became as regular as Mr. Carbuncle's after-dinner brandy. Eventually Jules stopped opening his mouth. And as he grew older, he never made a sound, at the dinner table or away from it.

William, on the other hand, became glibber and glibber. After a few months he began to imitate Morris.

"May I have the end piece, please?" William would say. "And gravy on everything?"

Once, however, he imitated Morris too closely.

"May I have more hollandaise, Pa?" he said, handing back his plate.

On this occasion Mr. Carbuncle's face, hovering over the steaming dish of asparagus, darkened dangerously. Horrified, Mrs. Carbuncle corrected William's presumption.

Since Jules never answered when asked what he cared for, he was given slender, often meatless servings. As time went by, William found himself with less and less appetite for the meat his brother went without, and eventually he began to refuse meat himself.

They hardly grew at all. Mr. Carbuncle, being a gentleman of leisure, spent most of his time at home, and as the years passed, the sight of two such puny things became positively offensive to him. Finally Mrs. Carbuncle moved them from their bedroom up to the attic, where they would be more out of sight.

At the dinner table Mr. Carbuncle would shake his head sadly, noting the number of cushions they required on their chairs in order to reach the table.

"And one of them dumb as a post to boot," he would sigh. "What did we do to deserve it, Amelia?"

But she had far too much respect for her husband ever to remind him that he had once referred to them as a golden opportunity.

. . .

On one of the top shelves was a musical instrument

the roof, his hands clapped over his ears

William, on the other hand, rarely b
to go farther than to hide by the
mahogany secretary that stood on the l
the top of the stairs. Mrs. Carbuncle
were well known to him by this t
minute she might turn around and
on an errand to the grocer's. But eve
voice had died down, like a crow fl
the distance, William would rer
antique secretary, coming out and
it. The pediment resembled two
break, and on one of the top shel
cal instrument, strange and lo
glass doors, like something und

CHAPTER THREE

A FINE LINDEN TREE stood in the yard of the Carbuncle estate, its roots rivering over the lawn. The attic window—a little round window in the gable—gave directly onto this tree, and on sunny mornings the boys were awakened in their bed by the nervous sunlight that jiggled in through the leaves. They would lie there and listen to the swallows that nested under the eaves.

Winters in the attic were less idyllic. It was unheated, and year by year the old cedar shingles were rotting off the roof, letting in more of the cold. Mr. Carbuncle, who had begun to speculate in gold, had long promised to reshingle. But the

promise remained unfulfilled, and to keep their blood circulating, the boys paced the attic in a huge astrakhan coat that Morris had discarded when astrakhan went out of fashion.

One winter Jules began to mope. William reminded him that the swallows would be coming back, but to no effect. Finally William convinced their aunt to let them move back down into one of the bedrooms. But Jules refused.

Spring came, and to William's dismay Jules failed to perk up. The songs of the birds, which Jules had always particularly loved, held no charms for him now. One perfectly nice morning he did not even get up for breakfast, and after the meal William went up to find him huddled in the corner under the slant of the roof.

"Feeling mopey?" William asked.

Jules shrugged.

Jules failed to appear at lunch as well. None of the three Carbuncles so much as noticed his

17

absence. After lunch William went up and found Jules still huddled in the same corner.

"Feeling fluish?" he asked.

Jules shrugged. William stared at him. Usually Jules's eyes were like two small blue pools, but now they looked empty, as if the plugs had been pulled.

When Jules was not at the dinner table that evening, William could not touch his food and excused himself before dessert, bent on discovering once and for all the cause of his brother's listlessness. He searched the upstairs for a pencil and paper for Jules to write with. But when he opened the top drawer of the mahogany secretary, the brass pulls rattled on the lower drawers. He had hardly found the box of paper when he got a whiff of disinfectant.

Mrs. Carbuncle came around the head of the staircase. "So now you're putting fingermarks on our finest piece of furniture. I thought as much when you skipped pudding. And what do you think you're doing with Mr. Carbuncle's stationery?"

"I want Jules to write down what's wrong with him."

"Really?" she said. "I didn't notice anything particularly the matter with Jules today."

"But, Aunt Amelia! He hasn't been down all day long!"

"Hasn't he? Well, I'm sure I wouldn't know about that—there isn't a peep out of him whether he's there or not. But I do know paper doesn't grow on trees. Stationery like that costs . . . Look at me when I'm speaking to you!"

She saw what he was staring at, and then she sighed, pulling a key from a pocket of her apron.

"I've seen you ogling that before," she said. "Will you keep your fingermarks to that if I give it to you?"

William nodded, speechless. She unlocked

one of the high glass doors and handed the strange musical instrument down to him.

"Mine?" he whispered.

"Well, it came with you."

William ran his fingers gently over the instrument. The wood was time-polished, and the strings were silver.

Mrs. Carbuncle turned to go down to her dinner dishes.

"Is it . . . a dulcimer, Aunt Amelia?" he asked.

She turned around, her eyebrows raised.

"How'd you know that?" she asked.

Soon he was alone. He sat down on the top stair with the dulcimer in his lap and ran his fingers over the sides of the instrument, which were inlaid with seagulls in mother-of-pearl.

There were two little cork-headed hammers tied by a slender thong to one of the dulcimer's pegs. Using one of these, he struck the silver

He sat down on the top stair with the dulcimer in his lap

strings. Morris, passing by on his way to lie down for the evening, made a sour face.

William stared down at the dulcimer in surprise, winding a finger in his nut-brown hair. He tried again, making sure the hammers struck the strings squarely. It sounded just as bad.

He began to fiddle with the pegs, changing the tuning of the strings. He tuned and tested, tested and tuned, losing all track of time.

At last he ran a finger over the strings like a harp and produced a sound that did not grate on his ears. Then, however, he found himself at a loss. The Carbuncles were not a musical family. He did not know a single song.

As he let the cork hammers wander over the strings, he had to smile at his luck. Almost immediately a tune began to emerge out of the random notes. It was simple but quite pleasing. He practiced it over and over and over.

Suddenly he heard the tinkle of ice. It was

the ice in Mr. Carbuncle's nightcap; his aunt and uncle were coming up to bed. It was ten o'clock, and since coming up after dinner, he had not once heard the grandmother clock at the end of the hall strike the hour.

He sprang up the ladder, the dulcimer under his arm. Only as he lowered the trapdoor behind him did he remember his brother.

Jules was sitting in the corner of the dim attic, his arms around his knees, his head hanging down, asleep. William set the dulcimer aside and carried his brother to bed. He hardly seemed to weigh a thing.

As he set him down, Jules woke up.

"Is your appetite back?" William asked, pushing back Jules's disheveled golden hair and feeling his brother's brow.

Jules did not seem to be running a temperature, but his eyes were still empty. William began to search for something to write with. But except for their bed, and a box of clothes, and the astrakhan coat hanging from a nail in the roof beam, the attic was bare.

Then he remembered what his aunt had said about paper not growing on trees. He opened the little round window, thrust his hand out into the night, and pulled in a bunch of new linden leaves. He took down the astrakhan coat and worked the nail out of the roof beam.

Sitting on the edge of the bed, he handed his brother the writing materials and asked what was the matter. Jules sat up. He took four leaves and scratched a word on each with the nail.

William stared at the message for some time.

He had spent every day of his life with Jules, but this was the first time Jules had spoken to him.

William looked from the leaves to the golden head, the hollow cheeks, the empty eyes. A solemn feeling came over him. His heart felt quivery. It was strange, sudden, as if wings were beating inside him. It was as if his heart were leaving him entirely.

The dimly lit attic was becoming unsettled. Things were running together like watercolors . . . he and Jules.

Wiping his eyes, William went over to get the dulcimer. He sat down on the bed again and struck the cork-headed hammers lightly on the silver strings. He began to sing.

"The one I love was like the tide
That runs under the quay,
Smoothing the wrinkles on the shore
Only to fall away.

"For the sea is dark and never still.
It never will obey
Hearts that are in the likes of me.
My love is gone away."

He sang the song to the tune he had practiced, singing in a clear, quiet voice as if he had known the words since the day he was born. When the song was finished, Jules's eyes were shining.

CHAPTER FOUR

WILLIAM MADE REMARKABLE progress on the dulcimer. He found he had a knack for making up songs. Before long Jules had several favorites. And when another winter came, the dulcimer could make them forget the cold.

One morning they were awakened by the first party of swallows arriving under the eaves.

But this spring turned out to be different. While the rest of Rigglemore grew brighter, the Carbuncle household only grew gloomier. The latest brands of tonic for baldness and the boxes of crisp cigars stopped arriving for Mr. Carbuncle from New York. Morris, feeling victimized at having his clothes allowance cut off, began to stay in bed on school days, asking to be brought elegantly bound books from the family library. One night, after drinking a lot of brandy, Mr. Carbuncle used his gold mining shares to light a fire. The next morning he hinted darkly that the family antiques, perhaps even the estate itself, might have to go under the hammer. Mrs. Carbuncle continued to clean.

One evening at dinner Morris unveiled a phrase he had gotten out of one of the elegantly bound books.

"Fiddling while Rome burns," he said, staring at William and Jules.

After this, when William and Jules came down to meals, Mrs. Carbuncle was wont to say, "Don't think we don't hear you playing that miserable music."

William hung his head over his plate. Up in the attic after the meal, however, Jules would

write him a message in leaves to the effect that his playing was not miserable at all.

One afternoon not long after Easter the town auctioneer paid the Carbuncles a visit. A dry, leathery old man, the auctioneer made a tour of the house, rapping pieces of furniture with his knuckles, fastening yellow tags onto brass handles, peering at the signatures on paintings, and speaking of the worth of everything in a voice so rapid that the words sounded like cards being shuffled. William and Jules, however, were not allowed to witness these curious proceedings for long. In the course of his appraisals the auctioneer naturally left many fingermarks, and needing to take her distress out on someone, Mrs. Carbuncle soon screamed at the boys to keep out from underfoot. So they went to sit under the linden tree, where William played suitably mournful songs on the dulcimer.

The sun had fallen below the roof of the

house when the auctioneer appeared on the front porch with the three sullen Carbuncles.

"Well, that's the lot then," he said as they started for the gate in the picket fence. "The truck'll be here tomorrow for the things. Sunup, so none of your neighbors'll be the wiser."

He stopped under the linden tree.

"What have we got here?"

"Our two objects of charity," Mr. Carbuncle replied.

"Not the youngsters. I mean that."

William stood up. "This is my dulcimer, sir."

"A dulcimer, is it? Why, it looks like a dandy. Let's have a gander."

William proudly handed over the instrument. The auctioneer ran his leathery hands over the time-polished wood and the silver strings.

"Don't see one of these every day," he murmured to the Carbuncles. "Looky here, mother-of-pearl down the sides as pretty as

you please. Yes, siree, all dressed up and nowhere to go."

"You don't say," Mr. Carbuncle said, brightening a little. "It's not worth anything, is it?"

"Not more'n four or five hundred—if a body knew how to talk it up."

"Really! Did you hear that, Amelia? Perhaps these tykes can earn part of their keep, after all. They've been something of a burden to us over the years, you know."

"Oh, I know," sighed the auctioneer. "All Rigglemore speaks of your charity."

Mr. Carbuncle, now almost cheerful, watched complacently as the auctioneer fastened a yellow tag around one of the instrument's pegs. William looked on in stunned silence.

"But it's mine!" he finally cried, finding his tongue.

Mr. Carbuncle, taking the dulcimer, had

little trouble holding it out of William's reach. Mrs. Carbuncle sighed.

"Think of it—raising his voice like that to his benefactor."

"A sad business," said the auctioneer, wagging his head.

Morris chose this moment to unveil another phrase from one of the elegant volumes.

"Ungrateful children are sharper than serpents' teeth," he announced.

"Yes," Mr. Carbuncle agreed. "A most ungrateful, ungentlemanly business."

Mrs. Carbuncle whisked the dulcimer off into the house. Mr. Carbuncle magnanimously walked the auctioneer all the way to the gate.

"Until dawn then," he said.

When he turned back to the house, he paid no attention to William tugging on the tails of his smoking jacket. Nor did he pay any attention to the desperate pleas that dogged him around the house. But when they sat down to a New England boiled dinner and William had still not let up, Mr. Carbuncle lost his equanimity.

"I'm in no mood for this," he said. "My furniture is covered with tags. My house looks like some kind of shop. But I ask one small sacrifice of you, and what do I get? Sniveling."

"There now!" said Mrs. Carbuncle, as if just what she had expected had happened. "You've ruined Mr. Carbuncle's digestion with your selfishness. Go up to your room this minute."

William excused himself, having not even touched his dinner.

When he was halfway up the ladder to the attic, he felt a tug on the cuff of his pants. He looked down and saw a golden blur.

Jules had followed him from the table. He seemed to be pointing at something.

William climbed back down and wiped his eyes. Jules was pointing at the high glass doors of the mahogany secretary, behind which lay the dulcimer. It looked stranger and lovelier than ever before.

William reached up and tried the latch. The glass doors rattled, locked.

They both stepped back, smelling disinfectant. Their aunt was standing at the top of the stairs, her arms crossed over her apron top.

"The one thing Mr. Carbuncle didn't have it in his heart to part with and you have to smudge it," she said. "Didn't I tell you to get up there?"

She pointed to the ladder. But William was now entranced by the dulcimer, shimmering behind the watery glass.

"William, didn't I tell you to get up there?"

He still failed to acknowledge her. She took him by the shoulders. He turned and looked at her blankly.

"Why, you'd think I was talking for my health!" she said as she pushed him toward the ladder. "Now get up, and don't let me lay eyes on you before breakfast."

Soon he was lying at his brother's side in the dim attic, staring up at the slant of the roof. On the floor below, the grandmother clock struck the hours. At ten he heard their aunt and uncle trudge up to bed. Then the silence of the house was disturbed only by the loose, rotten shingles, flapping on the roof in the wind.

After midnight a cold blade of moonlight came in the little round window. William slipped out of bed. Jules, rolling over quietly, watched his brother disappear through the trapdoor.

William stood before the mahogany secretary. Slowly he lifted his hands to the glass doors that glimmered in the moonlight from the window on the landing.

He recognized the muffled sounds of his aunt's and uncle's snores: one a high, thin sound, the other a deep, grunting wheeze. Bending down, he eased out the bottom drawer of the secretary. It creaked. He withdrew a brass candlestick from the drawer and then used the drawer as a step, standing on it.

He hardly had to touch the glass with the candlestick for it to shatter. As the pieces showered down onto the floor, a little triangle of the broken glass fell into his shirt pocket. He grabbed the dulcimer.

A doorknob turned, and then he smelled disinfectant. As he leaped down off the drawer, his aunt uttered a piercing cry. Then something huge and dark floated down from above, settling over his shoulders like a cape.

His aunt ran at him, screaming like a crow. He fled down the stairs and out the front door into the moonlit yard. His aunt was at his heels. Suddenly she shrieked. He looked over his shoulder and saw her lying facedown on the

The tails of the huge astrakhan coat flapping out behind him like wings

ground. She had tripped on one of the linden roots that rivered up on the lawn.

It was all he needed. He raced through the gate in the picket fence and down the hill, the dulcimer under his arm, the tails of the huge astrakhan coat flapping out behind him like wings.

CHAPTER FIVE

A DROP OF COLD WATER landed on his cheek, and he thought, The roof's leaking again.

Yet the bed felt curiously hard, and the air was not fusty, as it was in the attic, but cool and wild.

William rubbed the sleep from his eyes. Instead of roof beams there were the lordly boughs of pine trees high above him, higher than the ribs on the ceiling of a church. It was before dawn. The pieces of sky that showed through the trees were the color of his aunt's pewter dishes.

A shiver of memory went through him. He had broken the most treasured Carbuncle antique, stolen the dulcimer, and run off like a thief in the night, he knew not where.

He sat up and looked around. He had slept between two bulged-up roots, the astrakhan coat pulled over him. The forest was deep. The only sounds were the creaking of the high boughs in the breeze and the faint patter of dewdrops on the pine needles.

He was trembling. To calm himself he pulled the dulcimer from under the coat and began to pluck it. Its peaceful notes wandered out among the pines.

Suddenly the whole forest came alive with sound. His fingers froze; he lifted his eyes to the boughs above. All the birds in the forest seemed to have awakened at once: they were warbling, chirping, whistling, and singing. In a moment, however, the symphony of sound died away, leaving only the creaking of the pines.

William resumed his playing. The birds started up again. He stopped, experimentally. They stopped. He started again, and the forest resounded.

Soon the sun rose in the sky, spangling the pine needles with gold. William's trembling was quite gone now. In fact, it was nice to be somewhere new, serenaded by birds. After a while he stopped playing and began to wind a finger in his hair, his thoughts widening like ripples on a pond.

He stood up and shook the pine needles from his coat. A sheaf of leaves fell out of its pocket and began to scatter over the brown-needled floor of the forest. He dropped the coat and ran after them.

They were linden leaves, each with a word scratched into it. He laid them out between the two bulged-up roots.

He began to rearrange the scrambled leaves.

He found a number of messages, but they made grammatical sense only. Finally, however, he found the message, and his eyes shifted to one of the golden spangles. He saw an image of his brother, a golden figure crouched over the open trapdoor, while he, William, pressed his hands against the high glass doors of the mahogany secretary.

Slowly his eyes returned to the message.

with

THE

dulcimer

of

think

me

A solemn feeling had stolen over him. He had the sensation of wings beating inside him, and as he saw another image of his brother—this time huddled in the slanted corner of the attic, silent and empty-eyed and forgotten—the colors of the forest began to melt together before his eyes.

William stuffed the leaves back into the coat pocket and tucked the dulcimer under his arm. As he ran, his feet padded quickly and softly on the needled ground. He wove his way through the high-waisted trees.

But he had skipped dinner the night before, and long before he found his way out of the forest, the tails of the coat began to drag heavily behind him in the needles.

At last he emerged onto a meadowy down-slope. Hooding his eyes against the noon sun, he looked out over a quilted countryside of apple orchards in blossom and meadows spotted with gray boulders and black-and-white cows. There

46

was not a sign of Rigglemore or the hill above it.

He wandered despondently down the slope and across a number of bouldery fields, having to climb several stone fences. He heard faint music. He hurried over a knoll, then fell to his knees and touched his lips to a brook.

His thirst quenched, he noticed fish shadows darting across the water. He broke off a willow wand, undid a string from the dulcimer, and fastened it onto the end of the wand. With the silver string, it took only a moment to lure one of the fish to the bank. He dashed his hand into the water. Nothing.

He squinted up at the sky and sighed, seeing that what he had thought were fish were only the shadows of a flock of dark forest birds circling overhead.

But at least he was not lost. A stagnant river went through Rigglemore, through the mucky section of town. Assuming this was the beginning of it, he put the silver string back into his instrument and started downstream for home.

Little by little the music of the brook grew deeper. It became a stream. The stream widened into a river, and a road began to wind along the riverbank. William followed it, wrapping the dulcimer in the coat to protect it from the dust of the road.

He passed a number of people on the road, mostly farmers. One, the driver of a hay wagon, gave him a ride for a couple of miles and offered him a puff on his corncob pipe. William choked on the smoke, however, thinking of Jules. The rest of the farmers were a pithy bunch. None would commit himself on how much farther it was to Rigglemore; none had any food to give him; all eyed with suspicion the dark birds circling over his head.

It was painful to look at the cows in the meadows, chewing their cuds so contentedly. He fixed his eyes on the distance. Nothing looked familiar. But he noticed a strange, flat blue cloud forming on the far rim of the horizon.

By late afternoon he was weak from hunger. He tugged rather desperately on the coattails of fellow wayfarers, asking if this was indeed the way to Rigglemore. Many of them shook him off. A few replied, "Mebbe," or "Not as I know of." Most discouraging of all was the woodsman who laughed and said, "But you're not wriggling now, lad—why do you want to know the way to wriggle more?"

Finally, as dusk stole over the countryside, William became conscious of a roaring in his ears. This was a bleak sign. After a few more steps he collapsed on the roadside.

He lay on his back, staring up at the twilit sky. It came as little surprise to him that he should be seeing things: white things, circling among the dark forest birds overhead. Yet blinking only brought the hallucinations into sharper focus.

Suddenly he sat up and unwrapped the dulcimer. He stared from the mother-of-pearl seagulls inlaid along the sides to the white things in the sky. They were identical.

Somewhat revived, William got to his feet and continued along the road beside the river. The roaring in his ears grew louder, and in less than a quarter of a mile he found himself standing on the edge of a promontory. The river plunged over it—a roaring waterfall.

There was a broad plain below, and to William's surprise there were a number of rivers winding their ways across it; he had not imagined there were more than one. Beyond the plain lay the flat blue cloud that had captured his attention earlier. It went on forever in the evening light, its dark surface shimmering with movement.

"Dark and never still," he murmured.

Beyond the plain lay the flat blue cloud

The rivers on the plain below all finally merged and entered the dark expanse of a great harbor, around which was built a city that looked a hundred times the size of Rigglemore. William set off down the steep road, his eyes on a beacon that swept the sky from a lighthouse at the harbor's mouth.

He entered the great city on a wide, elm-lined boulevard. Facing each other across the boulevard were fine, stately houses with balconied rooftops, standing in rows like the elegantly bound volumes in the Carbuncle library. It was the hour when lamps were being lit: through bay windows he saw crystal chandeliers and mantelpieces displaying ships in bottles. But it was also the dinner hour, and as he passed along, he smelled food. Ham with raisin sauce. Sausage and baked beans and hot brown bread. Rack of mutton. Codfish and boiled potatoes in melted butter.

Finally from an ivy-covered town house came the smell of roast beef and Yorkshire pudding. His will defeated, William walked up the steps and knocked.

The door was opened by a butler in tails and patent leather shoes.

"Excuse me, sir," William said, "but I'm lost and—"

"Indeed you are." The butler nodded. "This is Park Row, not Pawn Street."

William hastily combed his fingers through his sweaty, dusty hair.

"But you see," he said, "I've come an awfully long way and I smelled—"

"You're quite right." The butler nodded again. "You do smell."

The door closed in his face. Turning away, William continued down the gracious boulevard. He asked the first person he met the way to Pawn Street.

53

"Down that way, then down around there," he was informed.

These directions took him across a bridge, past a great university, across another bridge, past a domed statehouse, and finally into a quarter where the streets were oily and lined with neither elms nor street lamps. The air had turned dark and briny. The gutters were littered with fishheads and oyster shells. Soon he found himself leading a file of alley cats, who seemed to be taken with the birds flying over his head.

He turned onto Pawn Street, which ran along the wharves. Here and there squares of yellow light fell onto the street from the windows of cheap hotels, giving the oil on the street a sinister sheen. There were noisy, dimly lit taverns as well, but when he peered in the windows, he saw countless glasses and tankards but not a single plate. Finally he collapsed in the gutter. He raised his head out of the refuse, took a last look at the mangy cats with their greedy yellow eyes, and passed out.

He dreamed that he was swimming in a great vat of clam chowder. It was very realistic; in fact, he could actually smell it. He opened his eyes and saw the open doorway of a seedy-looking establishment across the street: The Tumble Inn, according to some flaky lettering. He got up and followed the smell of clam chowder through the doorway.

It was not crowded like the taverns up the street. The only customers were a few sailors seated at round tables. None of them noticed him, for they were all staring at a lady in a short dress who was singing squeakily and wiggling on a little, well-lit stage. He could now smell minute steaks and seafood platters as well as clam chowder.

Opposite the little stage was a bar tended by an innkeeper with moist eyes and a droopy moustache. A door swung open at one end of the bar. A waitress with a tray of food and drink plodded across the sawdust floor to one of the round tables.

William went over to the bar and peered over the polished counter at the innkeeper.

"Excuse me, sir, but I've lost my way and haven't eaten since yesterday lunch, and I've come so terribly far."

"Come again?"

William repeated his little speech.

"Where are you from?" the man asked doubtfully.

"Rigglemore, sir."

"Come again?"

"Rigglemore, sir."

"Never heard of her," the innkeeper sighed. "I don't suppose she's much of a rig."

"Not a rig, sir. Rigglemore. It's a town."

"Ah. I figured she wasn't much."

William watched a waitress plod out of the swinging door with another tray of food. The innkeeper, with his moist eyes and droopy moustache, could not have been less intimidating, and William asked right out if he might have something to eat.

"Wait." The innkeeper pulled a cork bottle stopper out of either ear. "Now then, come again?"

"I was just wondering, sir, if you might please let me have something to eat."

"Well, it isn't much of a menu," the innkeeper said doubtfully, handing him one.

"Oh, but I'd like anything!"

"Well, some say the flounder's digestible. That's the special tonight—only two bits."

"Oh," said William. "But I haven't got two bits."

"Try the clam chowder then. It's only a nickel, and a side of crackers comes along for nothing."

William felt in his pockets. All he found was the little triangle of glass from the broken secretary.

"But I haven't got a nickel, sir. I haven't got a penny."

The innkeeper nodded, taking this information in stride. He cast a beleaguered look across at the squeaky lady singer and then started to replug his ears.

"But can't I have anything?" William cried.

"I don't suppose you're any good at washing dishes," said the innkeeper, one ear still open.

William shook his head sadly, thinking how jealously his aunt had always guarded her dirty dishes.

"I could sweep the . . ."

But the floors were covered with sawdust. The innkeeper lifted the other bottle stopper.

"Sir!" William cried. "I'll trade you my coat for dinner—it's too big for me anyway."

Unfolding the coat, William set the dulcimer on a bar stool and handed the coat across the counter.

"Astrakhan." The innkeeper nodded, as if he had expected this. "That's been out of style for ages."

He handed it back.

Then he said, "What do you have there?"

Starved as he was, however, and even though there was something rather appealing about the hopeless man, William could not forget the last time he had handed over his dulcimer. He put it under his arm and replied, "Only my dulcimer, sir."

"Dulcimer? What's that?"

"A musical instrument, sir."

"Ah. I don't suppose you play it very well."

"My brother likes my playing, but my aunt says it's miserable."

"Miserable." The innkeeper nodded.

He then turned his eyes toward the open doorway. Dancing on the threshold, wings flapping, squawking, was a flock of various kinds of birds.

"Now where do you suppose they came from?" he said wonderingly, tugging on his droopy moustache.

"Some from the forest, sir, beyond the meadows."

"Some from the forest? How do you know?"

"They came with me, sir. They've been watching over me or something."

"Watching over you or something? Why on earth would—"

A throat cleared. A sailor emerged from the shadow behind the door and pointed at the birds.

"Want 'em out, sir?" he said in a raspy voice.

The sailor had a forbidding aspect. His neck was purplish and grizzled; his head twisted a little to one side. Yet he addressed the moist-eyed innkeeper with the greatest respect and, at the innkeeper's nod, shooed the birds out of the doorway.

"But why should they be watching over you?" the innkeeper continued.

"I don't know," William replied. "They've just been following me around ever since I played in the forest this morning."

"Following you?"

A subtle change came over the innkeeper's face. The moistness left his eyes, as if for an instant they had hardened.

"That caterwauling." He sighed, casting another glance at the lady singer. "I can't hear myself think."

He cocked his head, and William went around the bar and followed him through the swinging door into a kitchen. The kitchen was full of lovely smells. But the innkeeper led him through the lovely smells into a little back office and closed the door.

"I don't suppose," the innkeeper said, leaning back on an untidy desk and rolling the cork stoppers in his fingers, "you're very good on that thing. But let's have a listen."

"If you like," said William.

He sat in a chair in front of the innkeeper, tuned the dulcimer, and played a song of hopeless love. When he had finished, he looked up from the silver strings. The innkeeper was staring over his head at the office wall, as if at a beautiful painting. William looked around. The wall was bare except for a little calendar.

The innkeeper stared there so long that William began to feel ill at ease. But then the man looked down, staring from William's face to the dulcimer in his hands.

"Well," the innkeeper said slowly. "Well."

"May I please have something to eat now, sir?"

"Where on earth did you ever learn to—What did you say? Eat? Yes, of course. But just wait a little minute."

He rummaged around on the untidy desk until he found a certain long sheet of paper.

"Well, now, you'll play for me again later? I'll bet you're hungry, aren't you?"

"Yes, sir," William replied.

Near the top of the document, where it said: AGREES TO PERFORM, the innkeeper wrote: YES. Then he glanced at the calendar again. It was May 12.

"Well, now, today's May eleventh, isn't it? Now let's see. Did you say you hadn't eaten since yesterday lunch?"

"Yes, sir."

So on the long sheet of paper, where it said: AGREES TO PERFORM UNTIL, the innkeeper wrote: MAY 11.

"Well, now. Will you sing for your supper?

And speaking of that, how would you like pork chops with apple dumplings? Do you care for dumplings?"

"Oh, yes, sir!"

So on the long document, where it said: WAGES, the innkeeper wrote: WILL SING FOR HIS SUPPER.

"That's settled then. Just sign there at the bottom and I'll have the cook put the dumplings on."

William could not think why he should have to sign his name for the cook to put the dumplings on. But he did it eagerly all the same, taking the pen and scrawling *"William"* where the innkeeper pointed.

"Fine," the innkeeper said. "And now the last name."

"But I haven't got a last name, sir."

"Don't be absurd," said the innkeeper. "Everyone has a last name. Without a last name, there might not be any dumplings."

William began to wind a finger in his curly nut-brown hair. The connection between his last name and dumplings was obscure. The innkeeper, too, seemed mysterious, having lost the appealing moist look in his eyes altogether.

Suddenly the innkeeper opened the office door, letting in the smells from the kitchen. William signed *"Carbuncle"* after *"William."*

"Carbuncle," the innkeeper said thoughtfully, looking at the document. "I'm afraid that won't do. Not the least bit catchy. . . . What was it you called that thing?"

"My dulcimer, you mean?"

"Dulcimer, dulcimer, dulcimer," the innkeeper said. "Dulcimer. Around here we'll call you the Dulcimer Boy."

William shrugged. He could not have cared less what he was called around there. As soon as he ate and had a nap, he would be setting out to get back to Rigglemore.

Soon a plate of pork chops and steamy dumplings was set before him on a tray. He skewered a dumpling. But then for a moment he simply inhaled the smell, wondering if perhaps Jules, too, had not eaten all that day.

CHAPTER SIX

H E WOKE IN A hammock. It was strung up in a little box of a room with sunlight leaking in between the boards on one wall. And there was a strange lapping sound, like a great heart beating nearby.

He dimly recalled falling asleep after eating. He had the uneasy feeling that he had taken more than a nap. Swinging out of the hammock, he peeked through one of the sunny cracks.

The room seemed to be in the back upper story of the inn, on the side that did not face Pawn Street. Down below, waves were beating against the foundation.

It was long and lovely, the sea. It stretched out beyond a harborful of ships and boats, out to where the ridges of the incoming waves were slender silver streaks in the morning sun, like the strings of his dulcimer. He turned and saw that the dulcimer was under the hammock, sitting on the folded coat. He gathered them up and went to the door. The door, however, was knobless.

He pounded on it. It opened almost instantly. In the hallway stood the sailor with the purplish, grizzled neck and the head that was askew. With the pleasantest smile he could manage, William slipped out of the room and down the back stairs.

The inn was deserted except for the innkeeper behind the bar. All the chairs were stacked upside down on top of the round tables, and the sun was shining through the dirty windows onto the sawdust floor. William went up to the bar.

"Good morning, sir. Thank you very much for your hospitality."

"Good morning."

William offered his hand over the counter, and the innkeeper shook it.

"I do hope we'll meet again, sir, so I can return the favor."

He turned to go. But the grizzly-necked sailor, who seemed to have followed him downstairs, had sidled into the doorway.

The innkeeper came around the bar.

"Only piece of luck I ever had," he said. "Ah, I see you've noticed his neck."

William looked elsewhere.

"Found him hanging from a tree out near the lighthouse. When I cut him down, he was still breathing, and he's been loyal as a dog ever since. Never would tell me what he'd done, though." The innkeeper lowered his voice. "Between you and me, I lock the cash register at night."

69

The innkeeper cocked his head, and the half-hanged sailor stepped obediently aside.

"Well," William said as they walked out, "I do hope we meet again."

"Oh, we will. Several times a day."

William squinted at the iridescence of the oily street in the sun.

"Really? Are you traveling to Rigglemore, too?"

"No, I'm afraid I have to stay here and innkeep," said the innkeeper. "I wanted to show you my handiwork."

He pointed to a freshly painted sign on the curb. It read:

THE DULCIMER BOY

PERFORMING NIGHTLY

~ *Shows at 8, 9, 10, 11,* ~

and Midnight

William stared from the sign to the inn-keeper's face.

"But I'm leaving."

"No, I'm afraid not." The innkeeper sighed and proceeded to explain that William had signed a contract running until May eleventh, which was a year minus two days away. "But you're perfectly free till eight o'clock. Get some breakfast in the kitchen, go back to bed, practice your instrument—do whatever you like."

William took the last piece of advice. He darted off down the oily street. He had not gone a block, however, before the half-hanged sailor caught up with him and plucked him up by the scruff of the neck.

William cried out at the top of his lungs. When he was set down again in front of the inn, he felt the street trembling beneath his feet.

An awesome horse had galloped up, a

chestnut that must have been twenty hands tall. William, flanked in the doorway by the inn-keeper and the half-hanged sailor, stared in silence at its huge, flaring nostrils.

"Trying to scuttle off without settling up, is it?"

William craned his neck to one side. Atop the fabulous horse a small, ruddy-faced police-man was perched.

The innkeeper stepped forward and stroked the horse's neck.

"Only my new performer trying to run out on his contract, Johnny," he said.

"Contract?"

The innkeeper ducked into his inn. He returned with the long document William had signed, and a tankard of ale, both of which he handed up to the policeman.

"This your John Hancock on here?" the policeman asked William.

"I suppose so, sir. But I still have to get back to Rigglemore."

"Do you?"

"But of course he can't," the innkeeper put in, taking back the contract. "He signed his name."

"You signed your name," said the policeman.

"But he said next year!" William cried. "My brother will lose his spirit and starve to death in the attic!"

"Really?" said the policeman.

"Still the law is the law." The innkeeper sighed.

"That's right," the policeman said. "The law."

He handed down the empty tankard and reached into a pocket. The innkeeper insisted it was on the house. In a moment William's anguished protests were drowned out by the hoofbeats of the departing horse.

Having no appetite, William spent the day in the little wooden box of a room upstairs. He divided his time between swinging slowly in the hammock and staring through the cracks at the freedom of the sea. At one point the fusty smell of the room reminded him sharply of the Carbuncles' attic, and he pounded on the knobless door. The half-hanged sailor opened it. William showed him the leaf message, but the half-hanged sailor was not touched.

Just before eight o'clock the innkeeper came to fetch him down. As on the night before, the inn was nearly deserted, all but three tables being empty. At one of them a young sailor was nuzzling a girl with bright red lips and cheeks. A fisherman with a wind-weathered face sat at a corner table, still as a statue. At another table a longshoreman with a scar across his forehead was swigging rum.

Staring through the cracks at the freedom of the sea

William sat on a stool on the little stage and watched the innkeeper return to his bar and the half-hanged sailor step back into the shadow of the door. He began to play.

The longshoreman with the scar on his brow began to mutter over the music.

"What is this? Where's the tomato?"

William, who always felt rather solemn when striking the silver strings, managed to ignore this. He played a seafaring ballad, and when he'd finished that, he glanced out at the young couple and played a love song.

But the longshoreman did not let up.

"Put him to bed," he muttered louder. "Bring on the goods."

He began to pound his bottle on the table, and William was forced to stop in the middle of his third song.

Suddenly the fisherman with the wind-weathered face rose from the corner table and stared calmly at the longshoreman.

"Says I to myself," the fisherman said, "I wonder how you came by that scar."

"Huh?" said the longshoreman, turning with a leer.

"Had your head cleaned out like a fish, did you, mate?"

The longshoreman's jaw dropped open. But although the fisherman was of an ordinary size, something about him, perhaps the dead-calm look in his eye, seemed to unnerve the other man.

"Whoever did it made a mighty good job of it, mate," the fisherman murmured, taking his seat again. "Otherwise you'd know fine music when you heard it."

After that the inn was silent except for William's playing. He played until it was time to take a break before the nine o'clock show. As he walked off the stage, the longshoreman with the scar was clapping as loudly as the others.

Six customers were there for the nine o'clock show. For the ten o'clock show there were more than a dozen. By eleven there were fifty. For the midnight show there was standing room only. The waitresses, used to plodding, were run ragged.

The next night the inn was packed by eight o'clock in spite of a cover charge the innkeeper had decided to take at the door. In between shows the sailors who had been unable to squeeze in shook their fists in the doorway and made threatening suggestions that everyone should take turns. But as soon as William walked back onto the stage, all heckling ended. A solemn hush fell over the seedy inn, and not even the clinking of glasses could be heard. Sailors stood silently outside in the street, listening to the ballads and the love songs, the sad and the sweet songs, songs of farewell and songs of adventure on the swelling seas. Sometimes William sang along with the dulcimer in his clear, quiet tone; sometimes he let the dulcimer sing alone. But at the end of every hour he sang the same song—the one that had come to him mysteriously his first night with the dulcimer.

After that second midnight performance the dockfront crowd refused to leave the inn, stomping their feet and clapping their hands for more. The innkeeper led his weary performer up the back stairs, confiding that his coin had finally turned up heads.

William had been granted writing materials with the knowledge that any letter he wrote would be read by the innkeeper before being sent. Alone in his room, he wrote to his uncle, reminding him to remember Jules up in the attic. When this was done, he addressed the envelope:

Eustace Carbuncle, Esq.
The Hill Above Rigglemore
New England

Then he curled up in the hammock. In spite of his exhaustion he had to cover his ears to sleep, for the clapping and shouting were still rising from the inn below and the street outside.

CHAPTER SEVEN

THE NEXT MORNING, William awoke from a
wonderful dream in which he was just outside
the Carbuncles' picket fence, about to enter the
gate. That night was much like the night before,
with the crowd spilling over onto the street. The
morning after, he awoke troubled, this time
from a dream in which he was sitting contentedly
on a little stage, playing the dulcimer without
giving his brother a thought.

One afternoon in the kitchen, while the
cook was preparing the evening's chowder,
William managed to slip into the trash can and
bury himself under the broken clam shells. The

half-hanged sailor, however, dug him out before the trash was taken to the street. Another day he slipped a stirring spoon under his shirt. Late that night, after writing his nightly letter, he inserted the spoon into a crack in the wall of his room and started to pry. The boards, however, creaked, and the half-hanged sailor came in and confiscated the spoon.

After a midnight show, when the crowd had risen for its ovation, William tucked the dulcimer under his arm and leaped off the stage. He tunneled his way through the forest of legs toward the door. But suddenly he was hoisted into the air. A pair of sailors had lifted him onto their shoulders. Everyone wanted to touch him. He began to be bounced from one set of shoulders to the next. He hugged the dulcimer, fearing for it with all his heart.

Suddenly he was safe in a pair of arms, the instrument unsplintered. He stared up into a wind-weathered face, the face of the fisherman who sat almost every night at the corner table. The man walked back to the bar, smiling calmly at the people in his way, and set him on a bar stool.

"Will you please take me away from here?" William asked.

"Away, matey? When you sing so lovely every night?"

The innkeeper came around the bar and thanked the fisherman for coming to the rescue.

Summer arrived. The audiences came earlier and earlier until the street outside The Tumble Inn was regularly crowded by five o'clock. The innkeeper raised the cover charge and spruced up the establishment, for now he was catering not only to sailors but to people from all over the great city: bakers, bankers, musicians from the New England Conservatory of Music, even ladies and gentlemen from Park Row. Finally The Tumble Inn was written up in the newspapers.

One evening in early September, when the talk along the waterfront was of hurricanes brewing far out to sea, a particularly salty crew pushed its way into the inn and managed to take over one of the back tables for the nine o'clock show. Their talk was rowdy. Their ship had just docked after six months at sea, and they had spent the afternoon distributing their pay among the Pawn Street taverns. Even after the nine o'clock show started, they called out loudly for more rum and for certain young ladies in the crowd to come join them. Hardly any of these ladies obliged, however, and other customers glared.

"Shut up," people muttered. "He's starting."

But this did not silence them. One sailor, who kept ordering Irish whiskey, went so far as to pull a well-rouged lady onto his lap and begin describing her beauty over the music.

By the end of the hour, however, most of this drunken crew had grown subdued.

Most of this drunken crew had grown subdued

"The kid can play a lick," one of them admitted.

A murmur of pleasure rose from the crowd as William started the familiar song with which he ended every hour.

> *"The one I love was like the tide*
> *That runs under the quay,*
> *Smoothing the wrinkles on the shore,*
> *Only to fall away.*

> *"For the sea is dark and never still.*
> *It never will obey*
> *Hearts that are in the likes of me.*
> *My love—"*

A glass, hurled from somewhere, cut the song short, striking William a glancing blow on the temple. He slumped forward over his instrument.

The audience stared at the stage in stunned silence.

Then the tumult began. The people in front rushed to the boy's aid, tossing the melted ice from their drinks into his face to try to revive him. The rest of the crowd immediately turned ugly. Sailors brandished knives in the air, calling out for revenge. All was confusion.

The wind-weathered fisherman did not move until he saw William come around. Rising from his corner table, he then pushed his way back through the angry mob. At the table taken over by the salty crew he saw one sailor still seated, flushed and trembling, a rouged woman staring up at him in shock from the sawdust floor. The fisherman pulled this man out of his chair and walked him through the crowd as if he were a friend who had had one too many. The clamor in the inn was growing fiercer by the moment; everyone was turning and accusing someone else. The fisherman, smiling calmly at the people in his way, walked the drunken sailor out the door and through the confused mass of people outside.

"Where you bunking, mate?" the fisherman asked.

The sailor pointed groggily up Pawn Street at one of the cheap hotels.

"Right you are," the fisherman said.

He walked the man up to the doorway of an establishment called the Seaman's Sling, where sailors slung up their hammocks for fifteen cents a night. Then he took his arm out from under the man's shoulder, and the sailor collapsed drunkenly in the gutter.

"I wouldn't be setting foot in The Tumble Inn again, mate."

The fisherman spoke the threat as if making a casual remark. He did not draw out the marlinspike he had in his belt.

"Why'd you go and do a thing like that anyway?" he asked.

"Why?" said the sailor, staring up with
bloodshot eyes. "Because that was . . . my song.
It was . . . my song."

The fisherman looked down at the drunk
curiously. Then he called for the hotel keeper,
who emerged with a sigh and pulled his guest in
by the wrists.

CHAPTER EIGHT

THE GLASS RAISED a bump like a quail's egg on the side of William's head, but the innkeeper decided it was not serious enough to lose a night of business over. So William performed the next night as always, trudging upstairs after the last show with the half-hanged sailor at his heels. In the hammock that night the throbbing in his head woke him again and again, sometimes from the dream that he was playing the dulcimer on the little stage, sometimes from the dream that he was outside the Carbuncles' picket fence.

One night later that week, after the ten o'clock show, a withered old gentleman got up from one of the round tables. A number of heads turned as he walked back to the bar, leaning on a silver-headed cane; several people murmured.

The innkeeper gave the counter a quick polish as the respectable old gentleman came up.

"Enjoy the show, sir?"

"Yes, indeed."

"Have I seen you somewhere before, sir?" the innkeeper asked uncertainly.

"I doubt it. I'm just in town on a visit. My granddaughter is starting at the university this week."

"Ah."

"I happened to read about the boy and thought I might come down and hear for myself. They couldn't do him justice in print."

The innkeeper nodded complacently and smiled his new smile, which always seemed rather at cross-purposes with his droopy moustache.

"You'd like one for the road then?"

The old gentleman shook his head.

"The boy certainly fetches a crowd. Would it be impertinent for me to ask what you pay him?"

The innkeeper gave his moustache a tug.

"Well, now, to tell you the truth, I'm the one who went out on a limb and gave him his start, so he sort of owes me. As a matter of fact, I took him in when he hadn't a penny to his name."

"You have a contract?"

"Oh, yes. It runs to May eleventh."

"Next spring! That *is* a long run. And a pity, too. . . ."

The old gentleman glanced around the inn and then pulled out his wallet.

"I have seven hundred and fifty dollars' traveling money," he murmured, and then, to the innkeeper's astonishment, produced that sum on the counter. "Would you consider parting with the boy's contract?"

The innkeeper swallowed, staring at the large bills.

But then the cash register, which had been ringing so regularly those past months, caught his eye. And beyond that was a long row of liquor bottles, all neatly plugged with their cork stoppers.

He shook his head.

"A pity." The old gentleman sighed, slipping the money back into his wallet.

The old gentleman hobbled out of the inn on his cane, accompanied by an attendant. The eleven o'clock show was starting as they made their way through the crowd outside. They walked up the dark street to the corner, where the attendant left the old gentleman and went in search of a vehicle.

While the old gentleman stood waiting by the curb, the cane was yanked out of his hand from behind. He found himself sitting in the oily street, staring up at a man with a twisted smile and a horrible, grizzled neck.

The half-hanged sailor, having witnessed the attempted transaction in the bar from his post behind the door, had shadowed the old gentleman up the street. The gentleman now struggled to get up, but the half-hanged sailor easily prevented him from doing so by poking him in the chest with his own cane. He then poked the bulge in his victim's suit coat, where the wallet was.

"I see," said the old gentleman. "However, I'm afraid I don't conduct business while sitting in the street."

"What about while you're dead then?" asked the half-hanged sailor.

Smiling his twisted smile, he raised the cane in the air. But as he did, the cane was yanked out of his hand from behind.

It was not the attendant but a scruffy seaman. Pulling a knife, the half-hanged sailor spun and made a lunge at him.

There was a harsh howl of pain. The seaman had sidestepped and brought the cane down in a crushing blow on the back of the sailor's neck. The sailor, clutching his neck, stumbled off down the dark street, rasping in agony.

After helping the old gentleman to his feet and restoring him his cane the seaman gave a silent nod and turned to leave.

"My dear fellow!" the old gentleman cried. "Not so fast, I beg of you! You've saved my life."

The seaman turned with a shrug and let the gentleman clasp his hand.

"Are you quite all right?" the old gentleman asked.

"It's not the first hole." The seaman shrugged, fingering the rip the knife had made in his worn sailor's blouse.

"May I ask your name?"

"Drake."

"Gildenstern." The gentleman smiled.

The seaman turned with a shrug and let the gentleman clasp his hand

"Well, sir, you must be the only sailor ashore who's not down listening to that lad. My luck."

Drake, who was the seaman the wind-weathered fisherman had warned never to set foot again in The Tumble Inn, turned and looked back down the street. In the silence of the dark, seedy quarter the two men listened for a moment to dulcimer music in the distance.

"That lad's going to make a name for himself. I did my best to get him for a Christmas concert, but to no purpose." The old gentleman smiled again. "Would you do me the honor of joining me for a late supper, Mr. Drake? There's a place near my hotel serves an excellent New York cut."

Drake looked from his scruffy navy-blue clothes to the old gentleman's suit, a gold watch chain looped across the vest.

"I'm busy," he said. "Sorry."

The old gentleman sighed. He then took a

card from his wallet and wrote something on it with a silver pen.

"Here's my card. I'll be very disappointed if I don't hear from you."

Horses approached. The old gentleman clasped the seaman's hand once more and then stepped into the vehicle with his attendant. Drake walked back to the doorway of the Seaman's Sling, from which he had witnessed the assault. In the light of the doorway he glanced at the card. He stared at it a minute and then slipped it into a frayed pocket.

"Excellent New York cut," he murmured with a faint smile, resuming his post in the doorway.

CHAPTER NINE

Until almost one in the morning Drake listened to the music in the distance. Then he went inside to his hammock.

The next evening he went to The Tumble Inn early and joined the fisherman at his corner table. The fisherman's face darkened at the sight of him. But Drake asked how he would have felt if he had had a strange woman in his lap and then suddenly heard the song he himself had made up on his wife's death.

"I never could . . . talk proper," Drake said in his sad, broken voice. "But I could always sing."

The fisherman began to understand. When

The next evening he went to the Tumble Inn early

William came out for his first show, Drake stared at the dulcimer with the inlaid gulls, and the fisherman looked from the scruffy seaman's curly brown hair to the boy's.

After the first show the two men began to talk about the boy. The fisherman confided that something the young performer had said to him had led him to wonder if he was really content.

When the second show was done, William saw the fisherman beckoning from the corner table. He went over.

"Take a seat, mate," the fisherman said.

"Thank you, sir."

The fisherman managed to get the attention of one of the harried waitresses.

"What are you having?" the fisherman asked William.

"A cup of tea, please."

"A cup of tea for him, and another Irish whiskey for my friend Drake. What's your name, lad?"

"William, sir."

"William, shake hands with Drake here."

William shook hands with the scruffy seaman. The fisherman took out a bit of scrimshaw and began to work on it. Drake, however, stared down into his empty glass in silence.

When the drinks came, the fisherman murmured, "You know, I could listen to you play till the last tide. But says I to myself, how can he play such sad songs when everyone's wild about him and he must be so happy?"

"Oh, but I'm not so happy!" William cried.

Given this rare opportunity to confide in someone, William spoke in too great a rush. His words came out in a jumble.

It was time for the ten o'clock show. William played his saddest songs, thinking only of Jules. After the show he glanced hopefully at the corner table. But the two men did not beckon him over.

Aided by Irish whiskey, Drake was revealing

his own history. He described how, being good for nothing but shipping out, he had taken his two young sons to his wife's sister when their mother had died.

"A fine old New England family, the Carbuncles."

"But why didn't you tell him?" the fisherman asked, shifting his eyes from the father to his son on the stage.

"I'm half a drunk," Drake said, staring into his glass again. "Sometimes I think I never should have given them up. I've been . . . thirsty ever since."

"But you've no reason to be ashamed, mate. And he has a right to know who he is."

Drake gave the fisherman a sober look.

"He doesn't need my name. He's making one for himself."

After the midnight show the two men joined in the clamorous applause. Half an hour later, when the inn had finally emptied, they made their way over to the bar, behind which the innkeeper was tallying the night's receipts.

"One more for the road, men?" the innkeeper asked.

"No," said the fisherman. "Just a look at the lad's contract."

"Now, that's a popular item this week." The innkeeper smiled at his faithful customer. "Don't tell me you want to make a bid?"

"Nope. Just want to look it over."

Eyeing the fisherman's disreputable companion, the innkeeper turned the key in his cash register.

"I'm afraid it's locked up for the night, gentlemen."

The fisherman shrugged.

"The lad signed it?" he asked.

"Naturally."

"How?"

"With his signature, William Carbuncle. How do you think?"

"'Tisn't his name," the scruffy seaman murmured.

"Come again?"

"'Tisn't his name," the seaman repeated, holding the innkeeper's eye. "His name's William Drake. So that contract of yours doesn't . . . hold any water."

The innkeeper looked a little shaken. While he stared at the speaker of these words, the fisherman went around the bar and through the swinging door.

In a moment the fisherman returned with the boy in his arms, the astrakhan coat and the dulcimer piled on top of him.

"What!" said the innkeeper. "You don't suppose you're going to kidnap my—"

"Shhh, he's asleep," said the fisherman.

The innkeeper, now genuinely alarmed,

turned and found the shadow behind the doorway empty.

"Tonight, of all nights, for him to be laid up!" he muttered.

He began to pull on his moustache, shifting his eyes to the fisherman.

"You've got a day trawler, worth a few hundred. I'll let you have him for— Wait!"

The two men walked out of the inn onto the deserted street. It was a moonless night. The fisherman transferred the boy and the dulcimer into the arms of the sailor.

"He half woke upstairs," the fisherman said softly. "He was fairly conked out, but when I ask if he wants to get back to those Carbuncles, he smiles. So good luck to you, mate."

The seaman stared over the dulcimer at the fisherman's wind-weathered face. Unable to find the right words, he gave the man a nod and then carried the boy away up Pawn Street.

The fisherman listened to the seaman's footsteps recede in the stillness of the sleeping waterfront. In a moment the innkeeper came out the door. He did not burst or stumble out, but walked out, strangely composed.

"Gone?" he said.

"Yup."

The innkeeper nodded. His eyes were moist, his shoulders stooped.

The seaman's footsteps receded into silence. Slowly the fisherman lifted his eyes. An unearthly rushing sound was stealing over the darkness.

The innkeeper sighed.

"I turn down seven hundred and fifty dollars, I give up my performer for nothing, and now it's one of those hurricanes coming in to get the inn."

But the fisherman, who knew the sea, shook his head.

"Birds," he said.

All he could think of was the boy in his arms

CHAPTER TEN

T HE SEAMAN HEARD the same noise overhead but paid it no mind. Nor did he really notice the steepness of the road leading up from the seaboard, nor the nip in the night air, nor even, when he had followed a river for many miles, the weariness in his legs and the heaviness of his breath on the dulcimer. Although he had been away from the salt sea air only once before in his life, he did not give it a second thought, never casting a backward glance. But when, after many hours, a shark-colored light began to seep over the sky and he saw that a great flock of dark and light birds was flying directly overhead, he realized he was inland, where things were unaccountable.

The sun rose at his back, and Drake picked up his pace. All he could think of was the boy in his arms, yet he dreaded the thought of William's waking before he got him home. The road finally veered off from the river. It skirted a vast pine forest. After passing through a boggy region, it picked up another, more stagnant river, eventually leading him to the outskirts of a town.

By this time the sun was well up. Drake, remembering his other visit, carried his bundle through the sleeping town and up the road winding onto the hill above it.

He stopped outside the gate of the first house after a blaze of maples. It was a grand old house with a linden tree in front, its leaves just turning gold, and brand-new cedar shingles on the roof. As he stared in over the picket fence, he thought how the boy and his brother had grown up there, going to bed every night in some snug room with white curtains, and he was reassured of having done the right thing by them all those years ago.

Drake set the sleeping bundle under the fence with care, placing the coat over the boy and the dulcimer beside him, then started off down the hill. But recollecting something, he stopped and walked soundlessly back. He slipped a card from a frayed pocket and placed it in the sleeping boy's hand. Then, before leaving for good, he bent down and kissed the boy's temple, on the place where it was a little black-and-blue.

William opened his eyes

CHAPTER ELEVEN

Willow OPENED HIS EYES and realized he was having his usual dream of waking outside the Carbuncles' picket fence. Reclosing his eyes, he tried opening them again to wake up properly.

This time he noticed slight variations on his dream. In the others there had never been birds perched on the pickets of the fence. Nor had the fence been freshly painted, nor the roof of the house newly shingled. Nor had he been holding a card in his hand.

He read the card, gave a dubious shrug, and slipped it into his pocket. He wound a finger in his hair. His hair was dewy.

He decided to play the dulcimer. If the birds started to sing, it would be like the time in the forest, which had not been a dream.

Leaning back on the fence, he took the dulcimer in his lap. A faint smell rose from it, the smell of Irish whiskey. He began to play. The birds on the pickets joined in like an orchestra.

He leaped to his feet and rushed through the gate to the front porch. As he knocked on the door, he decided that, whether his aunt and uncle had forgiven him for breaking the antique secretary or not, he would rush straight in and head for the attic.

"Why, good morning. I haven't seen you in a long time."

Smiling in the doorway was a plump gray-haired lady in a dressing gown. He recognized, to his amazement, the wife of the town grocer, who in the past had taken her turn working behind the counter in the store.

William glanced left and right. But there, unmistakably, was the linden tree, its roots rivering over the lawn.

"Ma'am?" he said. "Is Mr. Carbuncle home?"

"Mr. Carbuncle? Why, I'd give my eyeteeth to know where that man's got to. But I haven't seen hide nor hair of him since May."

William stared at her.

"The roof was in a shocking condition," she went on, "when he sold. First rain we had, it leaked into the attic by the—"

"The attic?" William burst out. "You've been in the attic?"

"If I had the mop up there once," she said with a sigh, "I had it up there a hundred times."

"Have you ever seen Jules? He has golden hair, and he can't talk, and he's even smaller than I am."

The lady shook her head and went back into

the front hall. Returning, she handed him a bundle of letters.

"I've never had a notion where to send the mail on."

William lost the color in his face. The addresses on the envelopes, all still sealed, were in his own handwriting.

The letters fell from his hands, and he turned and raced down the hill. His first thought was of the school on Elm Street. He flew up the granite steps, down a hallway full of shuffling, morning-faced scholars, and burst unannounced into the principal's office.

"Which room is Morris Carbuncle in?" he asked breathlessly.

The principal clucked his tongue.

"Morris, I regret to say, stayed back and has failed to return for the new year."

William rushed out of the school and down to Main Street. The shops were all opening for the day, and he began to go from one to the next, inquiring after the Carbuncles. In one shop a dressmaker stared at him and then exclaimed to her fellow worker, "Jenny, remember how I went to visit my cousin Frank, Jr., for five days and six nights over to the city the third week in June? Remember the musical concert I told you about?"

"Remember!" Jenny sighed.

"Look at this boy, Jenny. He favors the boy in the musical concert something wonderful."

But when he asked for the Carbuncles, William heard the same refrain in every shop: "Sorry, we don't deliver to them any more."

He stopped in at the grocery store, unable to imagine the Carbuncles stinting on food. The grocer knew William from his old errands and immediately dragged him into his new fine-foods department.

"Sardines, truffles, Camembert," he said

proudly in his faint foreign accent. "My son goes all over for me now—once every two weeks he drives the cart all the way down to New York City. Look—knackwurst, smoked herring, pumperni—"

"It's wonderful!" William said. "But the Carbuncles—don't they order food any more?"

The grocer shook his head.

William rushed out of the store and down Main Street. Old people always sat out on the shady side of this street, watching the world go by; William went from one of them to the next. But not one had seen a Carbuncle in months.

He began to wander the streets, the tails of his astrakhan coat dragging behind him. He wondered if the Carbuncles could have left the town entirely. He knocked on doors. A number of people thought he was selling something. The most helpful response he got from those who would listen was that they had heard of the name Carbuncle.

Finally the sun declined below the rooftops. Weary and disheartened, William sank down on a curbstone. The time-polished wood of the dulcimer showed him a vague reflection of his face. He saw himself as a betrayer and closed his eyes.

THINK OF ME. The words scratched on the old leaves seemed to scratch themselves on his heart. And then it was as if wings were beating inside him, as if that heart were leaving him entirely.

A strange, unearthly cry led his eyes skyward. The cry had broken from the flock of birds over his head. As their cry faded in the twilight, they flew away, deserting him.

He leaped up and ran after them, his shoes clapping on the street. But he could not keep up. Soon they looked like a swarm of gnats in the distance.

As he rounded a corner, he saw the birds settle on the roof of a three-story house at the end of the street. He gained ground on them.

Through the failing light he made out a tiny black silhouette, emerging from the chimney with a bag on its back. The tiny figure crossed along the peak of the roof, descended a long ladder, then started off down another street.

The birds mounted into the air and followed the figure, as did William when he reached the corner two minutes later. But night fell swiftly, moonlessly. The birds were no longer visible.

Through the darkness he heard the cries of children from the orphanage. The road made sucking noises underfoot. He was in the mucky section of town near the stagnant river.

Finally he sat down on a crate in front of the textile mill. When he caught his breath, he set the dulcimer in his lap and began to play. His song was answered by the birds, choiring from somewhere not far off in the night. He set off again through the dismal, slimy lanes, plucking the silver strings like a minstrel. The birds grew louder. At last he stopped, straining his eyes through the darkness.

And there they were, huddled on the roof of a shack.

The door of the shack cracked open. He stopped playing; the birds fell silent as well. The door opened suspiciously, the slit of candlelight widening little by little until the flickering shadow of light from within crept out over the place where he was standing in the lane.

A narrow silhouette appeared in the doorway.

"I thought that sounded familiar. Of course, we'd given you up for dead, but I see you're not."

Mixed with the slimy river smell was the sudden, sharp odor of disinfectant.

"No, Aunt Amelia, ma'am," William said, nearly tongue-tied.

"Oh, well then. So you've come crying back, have you?"

Through the doorway William had a glimpse of a small figure squatting by a bucket of water, washing chimney soot from his shaved skull. William stepped forward.

"Jules?"

The small, shaved figure spun around and stared out the doorway. Then, dropping his rag into the bucket, Jules flew past their aunt and embraced William, covering him with soot.

CHAPTER TWELVE

IT WAS A LARGE one-room shack with an oil-cloth window and peeling wallpaper. Light was provided by a few old candles leaning crookedly on shelves, and a smoky, smoldering fire inside a wood stove. In the middle of the room Mr. Carbuncle sat in an easy chair, smoking a cheap cigar. Morris lay like a large fish on one of two cots against the back wall. In a corner, looking peculiarly out of place, stood the antique mahogany secretary, the glass missing from one of its doors.

After Mr. and Mrs. Carbuncle had asked William a few perfunctory questions about his long absence, they began ignoring him as if he had never been gone. He sat on a threadbare rug in a corner, smiling at his brother, who was scrubbing rather futilely at the soot on his face and shaved skull. It was not a heartening sight, but at least he was alive.

His aunt began to make weary rounds of the room, flapping her apron in front of her. A dirty cloud of cigar smoke and smoke from the wood stove continued to hang below the ceiling, however. Her face grew more and more pinched. Finally, to William's surprise, she seized a newly lighted cigar out of her husband's mouth and tossed it into the bucket where Jules was washing.

William asked Jules about his hair. Jules turned to him with a melancholy look, still dumb.

"All it did was bring more soot into the house," Mrs. Carbuncle answered for him.

William looked in silent anger from her to his uncle. Breathing in chimney soot all day could be nothing for Jules but a continuous

Jules turned to him with a melancholy look

reminder of the ritual of the cigar smoke.

Soon Mrs. Carbuncle sat down at a deal table by the stove and began pounding some unsavory-looking meat with a mallet.

"Where do you shop, Aunt Amelia?" William asked.

"The grocery—where do you think?"

"But I asked the grocer if he still delivered to you when I was—"

"Then you must have asked for the Carbuncles," she said, giving the meat a sudden killing blow. "We've changed our names. We're the Joneses now."

When she had put some potatoes on to boil, she came over and pulled the dulcimer out from under his astrakhan coat. She went over to her husband in the easy chair.

"Busy?" she said sarcastically.

"Why, no, Amelia, my dear."

She thrust the instrument at the new Mr. Jones.

"Do you suppose you could manage to keep hold of that?"

"Of course, Amelia, my dear."

"Morris, will you track down one of those street urchins? Have him go and tell the auctioneer to send down anyone interested in buying a dulcimer. Here's a dime."

Morris lolled over and stared at his mother with a look of such doleful resentment that she finally gave a weary sigh and pulled on her galoshes.

As soon as she was gone, Mr. Jones had Jules fetch him a bottle of sweet wine from a wicker chest in a corner of the room. After a few drinks he began to tilt the dulcimer this way and that in the candlelight.

"Worth four or five hundred, if memory serves me."

William made a sound of protest.

"More, was it?" said Mr. Jones. "Then I'll have to keep it in a particularly safe place, won't I?"

This place turned out to be his lap. When Mrs. Jones returned and served up dinner, William watched his uncle instead of eating. Mr. Jones used the dulcimer as a tray. Yellow drippings oozed near the rim of his plate. And when he had finished his dinner, he lit up a cheap cigar, flicking the ashes carelessly here and there.

When Mrs. Jones had done the dishes in the bucket, she sighed wearily, dried her red hands on her apron, then went around the room, blowing out the candles.

"You can sleep with your brother," she said to William. "Jules, take out the garbage."

Once again she snatched away her husband's cigar, proving that Mrs. Jones had retained no trace of Mrs. Carbuncle's servility toward the gentleman she had married. He leaned back in the chair without protest and closed his eyes to sleep. Morris, meanwhile, was already sound asleep, drool running out the corner of his mouth onto his pillow. When Mrs. Jones had blown out the last candle, she collapsed on the vacant cot.

William lay waiting on the corner rug. It was some time before Jules came back in from taking out the garbage. The faint glow from the wood stove was dead, and the two boys lay together under the astrakhan coat in the dark.

An hour later, when their aunt and uncle had started snoring, Jules lit a candle stub that was wedged in a little crack in the wall, where the flame wagged in a small draft. He then spread out some willow leaves he had apparently collected on the riverbank while taking out the garbage. He began scratching words into them with a nail:

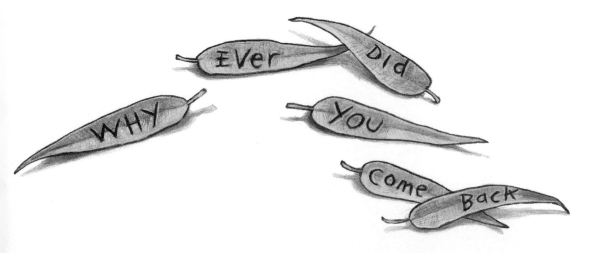

William looked curiously from the candlelit message to his brother's face. The answer was plain, but he dared not speak for fear of waking his aunt and uncle. He reached into the pocket of the astrakhan coat and brought out the old linden leaves. Although brittle, they were still legible. He arranged them for his brother.

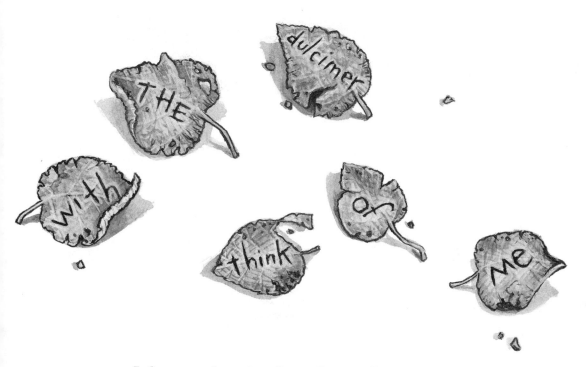

Jules stared curiously at the candlelit leaves.
He shook his head, and as he did, a few flecks of
soot fell from his shaved skull. He rearranged
the old brown leaves.

CHAPTER THIRTEEN

THE CANDLE FLAME began to dance. The draft grew stronger, rustling the brittle leaves. They swirled together like playing cards being gathered up after a hand, then the candle went out.

The darkness seeped into William's soul. Although still conscious of his brother at his side, he felt alone. One of the old leaves blew against his hand. He picked it up in the dark, closing his hand around it. It disintegrated into a dry powder.

Mrs. Jones shook him awake. A mouse-colored light had crept in under the door of the shack. The others were still asleep. She supplied him with a brush and bag and informed him that he was to learn chimney sweeping by cleaning out the stovepipe over the wood stove.

"Being small has some advantages," she said. "You've got a couple hours before I'll have to be warming Morris's porridge."

She opened the square cast-iron door and helped him into the stove, shutting the door behind him.

The bowels of the stove were in utter darkness. He felt around the foul bed of ashes, then groped overhead for the opening into the stovepipe. It was clogged. He took the handle of the brush and began to poke at it. Cakes of soot began to fall on him. The air began to taste like ashes; he choked. He beat his fist on the side of the stove. Then he collapsed in the heap of ashes.

He sputtered and opened his eyes. He was

lying on his back on the floor of the shack; Jules was pouring water on his face from the bucket. Mrs. Jones was standing over him, her arms crossed.

"How are you going to do chimneys if you can't even manage a little stovepipe?" she asked.

She turned to fixing breakfast. Jules pulled him back onto their corner rug and brought him a glass of water. William felt decidedly weak, but after drinking he could at least speak again.

"Uncle Eustace's pen," he whispered.

While Mrs. Jones stirred porridge, Jules sneaked over to the mahogany secretary and slipped a pen out of the top drawer. He gave this to William, who then pulled out the card he had found in his hand the morning before. William reread it dubiously. It had an embossed crest on it, below which were scrawled the words:

If I can ever be the slightest use,
I beg of you to get in touch with

Below which, in embossed lettering:

THE HONORABLE HENRY GILDENSTERN

MAYOR

THE CITY OF NEW YORK

William took the pen and wrote on the back of the card:

Please come to the shack by the river in Rigglemore, the one with the birds on the roof.

He slipped the card to Jules, telling him to give it to the grocer if he passed the grocery during the day.

"It probably won't come to anything, but his son goes all the way down there every couple of weeks," he said quietly, and then fell asleep on the rug.

Inhaling the ashes made William ill for five days.

"Just what I needed," Mrs. Jones said. "Another invalid."

Lying on the corner rug, William watched his brother come in every evening, covered with soot, handing his aunt the money he had made. The loneliness he had felt upon realizing that his brother was not utterly dependent on him began to disperse. Late one night he leaned up on an elbow and looked at his sleeping brother's shaved skull. It was faintly illuminated in the light of the quarter moon coming through the oilcloth, and he contemplated it without feeling pity.

He recuperated. His aunt insisted he finish the stovepipe before going out on a real job. In a leaf message Jules offered to do it for him late one night, but William refused. His next attempt, however, resulted in a relapse. He was ill for two more days.

Early on the morning of the third day he made yet another attempt, this time his aunt allowing the stove door to remain open for the sake of ventilation. He had worked his way about a foot up the clogged stovepipe when he heard the sound of horses in the lane outside. He crouched down into the stove itself, peering out the open grate.

There was a knock on the door of the shack. Mr. Jones, awakening with a start, shrank down in his easy chair.

"Someone we knew?" he said, horror-struck.

Mrs. Jones went and cracked open the door, letting a sheet of light into the dim room.

"Yes?"

"I'm looking for a Mr. Drake," a man's voice said from outside.

"Drake? There's no Drake here."

Mrs. Jones opened the door a little wider.

"The auctioneer didn't send you down to look at the dulcimer?"

"Dulcimer? You have a dulcimer?"

Pulling off her apron, Mrs. Jones opened the door all the way. A withered old gentleman hobbled in on a silver-headed cane.

Mr. Jones, struck by the man's respectable attire, got up from his chair.

"Good morning, my good sir. My name is Jones."

"And you've never heard of Mr. Drake?" the old gentleman said, looking around the dim room. "This *is* the shack with the birds on the roof."

"We come down here for the sport, every fall, to fish in the river," said Mr. Jones. "Our estate, of course, is on the hill above town."

The old gentleman hobbled up and took the dulcimer from his hands. Mr. Jones smiled.

"A fine example, isn't it?"

"Indeed."

"I believe it's valued in excess of six hundred dollars."

"Oh, no. Far more than that."

"More!" Mr. Jones contained himself. "My clumsy way of testing you." He stroked his bald head. "Out of curiosity, what would you call a fair price?"

"Price? Do you play, Mr. Jones?"

"Good heavens, no!" he exclaimed with dignity.

"Nor I," the old gentleman said sadly. "So in our hands I don't suppose it's worth much of anything."

Mr. Jones echoed the alarming words: "Not worth much of anything?"

William, at this moment, squeezed himself out of the stove.

"Finished?" Mrs. Jones asked.

William shook his head. Soot sprinkled down onto the floor.

"Mr. Jones," she said, "you're really going to have to do something about this mop of his."

Mr. Jones eyed the thick mass of sooty curls, a just perceptible gleam of relish in his eye. William wiped some of the soot from around his eyes and looked at the guest uncertainly.

"You won't let them sell it, will you, Your Honor?" he ventured after a while.

"Uneducated," said Mr. Jones. "Don't mind him calling you 'Your Honor.' He doesn't know any better."

"It's quite all right," said the old gentleman. "Is the dulcimer yours, son?"

"It came with me, Your Honor. Me and

You won't let them sell it, will you, Your Honor?

Jules." William looked around and pointed into the corner. "That's Jules."

The old gentleman reached out curiously and touched William's face. He began to wipe some of the soot from the boy's cheeks and forehead. His old eyes widened. Suddenly he looked rather angry.

"But good heavens! You're the lad who played in the inn!"

William nodded.

"But how could you be so careless with your hands?"

William looked down at his hands, encrusted with soot.

"I'm sorry, Your Honor, I was sweeping the stovepipe."

"Sweeping the stovepipe? With those hands?"

The old man had a surprisingly commanding voice, and as he spoke, Mrs. Jones shrank back a little toward the stove.

"Oh, are you responsible, madam? You have the good fortune, I take it, to be his mother."

"Only . . . only his aunt," she said in a voice not at all piercing.

Mr. Jones, however, drew himself up with dignity.

"Just who, sir, do you think you are," he demanded, "coming in here and cross-examining my household?"

The old gentleman gave him his card. As he read it, the pinkness drained from Mr. Jones's face. He stared aghast at the withered, distinguished features of the guest and then sank into his easy chair.

"You won't let them sell it, will you, Your Honor?" William said, repeating his original question.

"Have your aunt and uncle formally adopted you into the family?" asked the Mayor.

William shook his head.

"We're not real Carbuncles, Your Honor."

"Then they haven't any claim on you." The Mayor smiled. "That being the case, I don't suppose I could tempt you to make a trip to New York?"

"Your Honor?"

"Every year we give a series of free concerts, in different parts of the city, at different times of the year. The next is supposed to be the week before Christmas at the Opera House." The Mayor laughed. "Of course, you wouldn't be on the free end of things. We would pay you, say, a thousand dollars."

"A thousand dollars?" William looked inquiringly around the shack, from his cousin to his aunt to his uncle. "Don't you think that sounds like rather too much?" he asked them. "I mean, especially at Christmas?"

Morris was still sound asleep and made no reply. Mrs. Jones opened her mouth but was now unable to raise her voice to so much as an audible level. Mr. Jones, shrunken down in his easy chair, stared off at the empty wicker chest in the corner of the room, muttering something about a golden opportunity.

CHAPTER FOURTEEN

A FEW MINUTES LATER the old gentleman led William and Jules out of the shack into the morning light. Waiting for them in the mucky lane was a number of uniformed attendants, holding horses by their reins. Another attendant stood beside a gleaming carriage. The morning was sunny but crisp, and the Mayor quickly removed his greatcoat and draped it over Jules's shoulders. For a moment Jules was at a loss about what to make of such strange behavior. He took the coat off and tried to hand it back.

"No, no, you keep it," said the Mayor.

He then smiled at William, who was wrapped in his own coat.

"After your first concert," the Mayor said, "I've no doubt astrakhan will be back in fashion."

He walked to the carriage.

"Shall we be off?"

Jules, who had begun to stare at the Mayor with shining eyes, leaped immediately to his side, taking his cane for him and helping him up.

"There's room for two," the Mayor said, "if you'll do me the honor."

It took no more than this for Jules to climb up and sit beside him.

"Thank goodness!" the Mayor cried, delighted. "I have such a lot of room at home, and I've just lost my only grandchild to the university! Your aunt and uncle seem so attached to you I was afraid you might want to stay here with them and fish."

At the prospect of losing their sole source of income, the Joneses had demonstrated a deep,

The town chimney sweep was sharing the carriage

last-minute affection for Jules. But neither Jules in the carriage nor William, who had climbed onto a horse behind one of the attendants, gave the shack so much as a last look as they paraded off down the mucky lane.

The party attracted considerable attention as it rode through Rigglemore. Even the old people sitting out on the shady side of the street—even they, who had seen so much—could hardly credit their senses. Never had they laid eyes on such fine horses, such noble equipage, such splendid uniforms. There could not be the slightest doubt that the gentleman in the carriage that led the procession, carrying himself so well for a man of his age, was some great personage. But if this was so, how could it be that the town chimney sweep was sharing the carriage with him?

The party proceeded out of town along the stagnant river and then, after skirting a vast pine forest, entered the rolling countryside of woods and meadows. In a couple of hours, they came to a fork in the road where the horses naturally took the turning southward toward home. To the astonishment of all the others, however, William at this point slipped off his horse and bade them farewell.

Taken off his guard, the Mayor acted spontaneously. He stood on his authority and forbade William to leave them. But in spite of all the gratitude he owed the old gentleman, William only shook his head solemnly. He pointed to a flat blue cloud that had appeared on the eastern horizon and explained that with the help of a certain fisherman he hoped to find the man who had given him the Mayor's card.

"Ah, Drake," the Mayor said slowly, thoughtfully. "If I could take the time off, I'd like to look for that man myself. I owe him my life."

"Me, too, Your Honor," William murmured.

For just as William had known that the dulcimer was a dulcimer, and that the flat blue
cloud was the sea, so he had known from the
first that the scruffy seaman was more than a
scruffy seaman.

"When you come," the Mayor said, relent-
ing, "will you bring him for a visit? And do you
promise we'll see you inside of the month?"

William nodded. But even so, as he set off
down the road with the dulcimer under his arm
and the coat dragging behind him, a sadness
came into the eyes of Jules and the Mayor.

"I don't like to see him going off alone."
The Mayor sighed.

It was Jules, with his sensitive ears, who
heard the faint songs first. He lifted his eyes,
and then the Mayor lifted his. Accompanying
William, singing as they wheeled high over his
head, was a great flock of birds, dark birds from
the forest, white birds from the sea.

153

For Karen Russo
—T.S.

For Tamar Brazis
—B.S.

The Dulcimer Boy
Text copyright © 1979 by Tor Seidler
Illustrations copyright © 2003 by Brian Selznick
First published in 1979 by The Viking Press
Printed in the United States of America. For information address HarperCollins
Children's Books, a division of HarperCollins Publishers,
1350 Avenue of the Americas, New York, NY 10019.
www.harperchildrens.com

Library of Congress Cataloging-in-Publication Data
Seidler, Tor.
  The dulcimer boy / Tor Seidler ; illustrations by Brian Selznick.
    p.   cm.
  Summary: Twin brothers are abandoned on their uncle's doorstep in early twentieth-century
New England with nothing but a silver-stringed dulcimer.
  ISBN 0-06-623609-6 — ISBN 0-06-623610-X (lib. bdg.)
    [1. Brothers and sisters—Fiction. 2. Dulcimer—Fiction. 3. Orphans—Fiction. 4. New
England—Fiction.] I. Selznick, Brian, ill. II. Title.
PZ7.S45526 Du 2003   2001023875
[Fic]—dc21   CIP
                                                                              AC

Typography by Alicia Mikles ❖ 1 2 3 4 5 6 7 8 9 10